Weather is the condition of the atmosphere at a particular place over a short period of time

°C
°F
50
40
30
20
10
0
10
20
30
40
120
100
80
60
40
20
0
20
40

WEATHER ELEMENTS
(Clouds, Precipitation, Temperature and More)
2nd Grade Science Workbook
Children's Earth Sciences Books Edition

Speedy Publishing LLC
40 E. Main St. #1156
Newark, DE 19711
www.speedypublishing.com

Temperature is how hot or cold the atmosphere is, how many degrees it is above or below freezing.

Temperature s measured by a thermometer. Temperature is measured in degrees on the Fahrenheit, Celsius, and Kelvin scales.

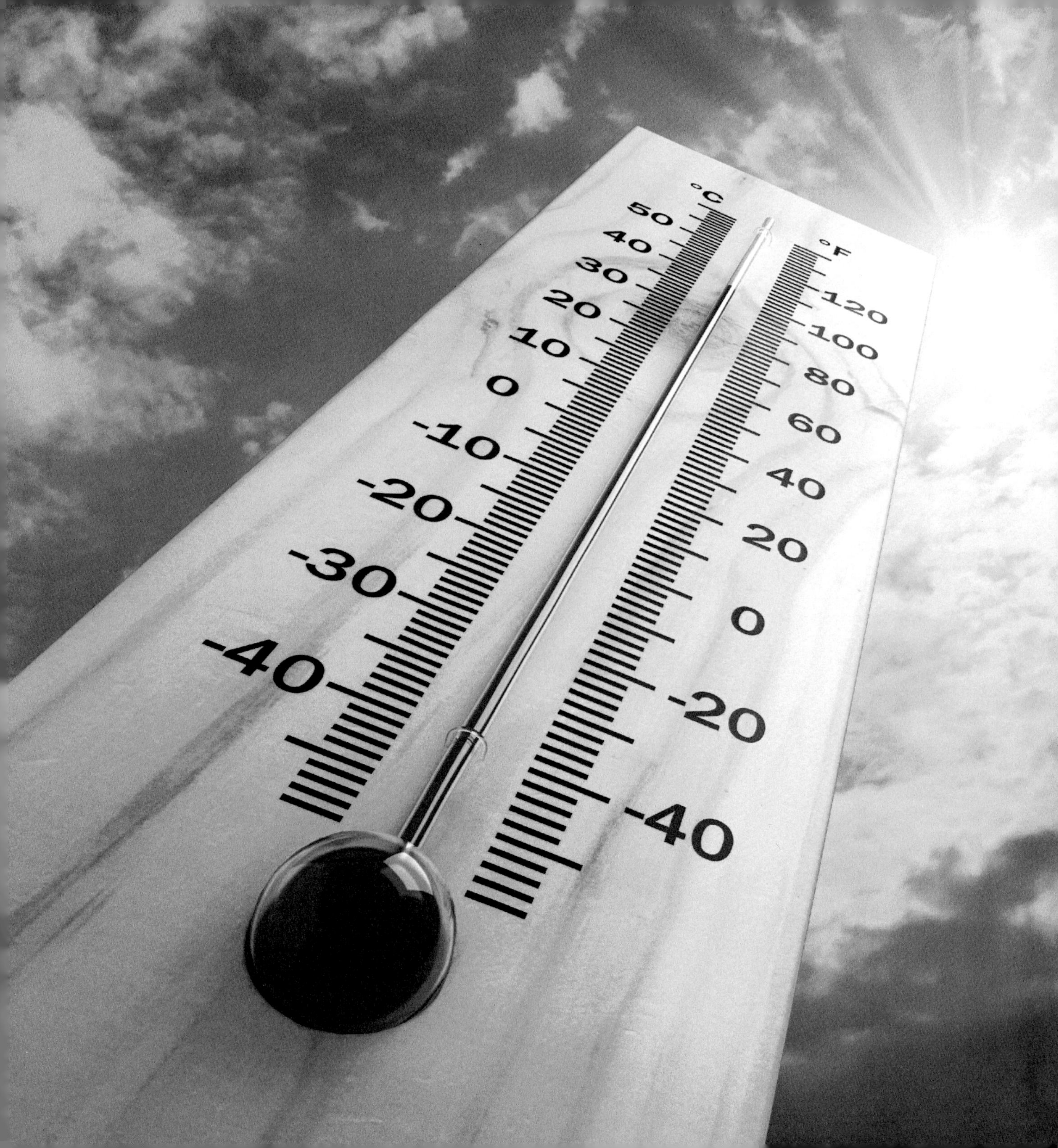
°C
50
40
30
20
10
0
-10
-20
-30
-40
°F
120
100
80
60
40
20
0
-20
-40

Temperature is also a measure of how fast the atoms and molecules of a substance are moving.

Wind is the movement of air masses, especially on the Earth's surface.

Winds are commonly classified by their speed, the types of forces that cause them, the regions in which they occur, and their effect.

The speed of that wind can be measured using a tool called an anemometer.

Humidity is the amount of water vapor in the atmosphere. Water vapor is the gas phase of water.

Humidity indicates the likelihood of precipitation, dew, or fog. Relative humidity is the most common way that we measure humidity.

Relative humidity, expressed as a percent, measures the current absolute humidity for that temperature.

Precipitation is the product of a rapid condensation process.

Precipitation forms differently depending on whether it is generated by warm or cold clouds. Major forms of precipitation include rain, snow, and hail.

มิลลิเมตร
200
190
180
170
160
150
140
130
120
110
100
90
80
70
60
50
40
30
20
10
0

Precipitation occurs when a portion of the atmosphere becomes saturated with water vapour.

Atmospheric pressure is the pressure exerted by the weight of air in the atmosphere of Earth.

1020
1010
1000
990
980
970
960
760
750
740
730
720

Meteorologists use a special instrument called a barometer to measure the pressure of the atmosphere.

770
760
750
1030
1020
1010
1000
990

In a barometer, a column of mercury in a glass tube rises or falls as the weight of the atmosphere changes.

A cloud is a large group of tiny water droplets that we can see in the air.

Clouds are formed when water on Earth evaporates into the sky and condenses high up in the cooler air.

There are
a range of
different types
of clouds,
the main
types include
stratus,
cumulus, cirrus
and nimbus.

Made in the USA
San Bernardino, CA
02 April 2017